It's Really Christmas

LILLIAN HOBAN

It's Really Christmas

GREENWILLOW BOOKS

New York

Library of Congress Cataloging in Publication Data

Hoban, Lillian.   It's really Christmas.
Summary: Born in the Christmas decorations in the
summer, a mouse whose generosity saves the lives
of all the mice in the attic but jeopardizes his
own is granted his wish to see Christmas.
[1. Mice—Fiction.   2. Christmas stories]   I. Title.
PZ7.H635It   [E]   81-6324
ISBN 0-688-00830-5   AACR2
ISBN 0-688-00831-3 (lib. bdg.)

1   2   3   4   5   6   7   8   9   10

FOR JULIA,
WITH ALL MY LOVE

CONTENTS

CHAPTER 1

SNOWDRIFTS · 9

CHAPTER 2

COTTON SNOW · 15

CHAPTER 3

SILVER TINSEL · 23

CHAPTER 4

REALLY CHRISTMAS · 31

SNOWDRIFTS

Gamey Joe was born early one spring in a box of tinsel that had been stored with the rest of the Christmas decorations in the attic of a big old house. His mother, Mrs. Mouse, wrapped him in cotton snow and hung a tiny spangled Christmas tree ornament over his head to keep him company while she took care of her household chores.

"Oh, isn't he dear?" cooed Aunt Hettie Mouse when she came up from the kitchen to visit. All the little cousin mice who had come up with her crowded round and stared down at Gamey Joe's pink little face and bright eyes.

"Hmmp," said Uncle Roger Mouse. "He looks like a Christmas present all wrapped up and ready to be sent.

You should have named him Christmas Joe instead of Gamey Joe."

"We almost did," said Mr. Mouse. "But since Christmas is a long way off, and Joe here has a bit of a game leg, we decided to call him Gamey instead."

One of Gamey's legs was a bit shorter than the others, and when he had grown a little, Mr. Mouse made him a crutch so he could run and play with all the attic mouse children. He liked to swing by his crutch from the rafters when they played Tarzan, and he liked to vault over the cobwebs, using his crutch as a pole, when they played hurdles. But most of all, he liked to lay his crutch aside, take the holiday decorations out of their box, and play Christmas in a corner behind the sofa by himself.

Sometimes he piled brightly colored ornaments on a bed of cotton snow and swirled silvery tinsel around them. Or he strung tiny jewel-like spangles on a red velvet ribbon that had come off a wreath. Once he made a tree of gilded pine cones and balanced an angel with gauzy wings at its top.

"Oh, Gamey, that is lovely," said his mother, who was

dusting behind the sofa. "It looks just like Christmas."

"When will it really be Christmas?" asked Gamey Joe.

"When mouse feet squeak on the frosty ground and snow drifts over the land and the brightest star of all shines in the sky," said Mrs. Mouse.

"I never *ever* had that yet!" cried Gamey.

"No, you haven't," said Mrs. Mouse. She hugged him and hurried off to make tea for some visiting mice.

Gamey Joe looked up at the patch of sky he could see through the window high in the gable end of the attic. "Perhaps the brightest star of all will shine tonight," he said. So all night long he stayed awake and stared up at the sky. But though he looked and looked, he couldn't tell which star was the brightest. "Perhaps mouse feet are squeaking on the frosty ground and I can't hear them," he said.

So all the next day he listened and listened, but he

couldn't tell if mouse feet were squeaking. "If only I could see out," he said, "at least I would know if snow has drifted over the land."

Gamey Joe climbed onto the brassbound trunk that stood beneath the window. He carefully pulled himself up on the chair that was balanced on the curved top of the trunk. Then he climbed up the slatted back of the chair, stood on his tiptoes, hooked his crutch over the windowsill, and hoisted himself up. Gamey pressed his nose against the window and looked out.

COTTON SNOW

Far below, he saw a garden enclosed by a sun-dappled wall. There were pink, violet, and lilac petunias nodding in their bed. There were ivory and red peonies, gold and orange marigolds, creamy white candytuft, and borders of blue bugle flowers. But nowhere, nowhere was there a single drift of snow.

"Oh," said Gamey Joe, pressing his nose harder against the window. "Not even the tiniest bit of snow...not even a snowflake!" Something moved on top of the wall. A large cat yawned and stretched, and turning, looked straight up at Gamey Joe.

Gamey was so startled that he ducked back from the window. His crutch fell on the chair, tipping it over. Crutch, chair, and Gamey fell to the floor with a crash.

"Well, well," said Aunt Hettie, who had just come up from the kitchen. "This certainly will not do!"

"No, it won't," said Uncle Roger, peering over her shoulder. "It's just what the people downstairs are making a fuss about. They say there is so much racketing and clattering and scampering up here, that there must be mice in the attic. You had better take warning," he said sternly to Gamey Joe. "If you don't stop all the noise and start being quiet as a mouse..." Uncle Roger paused and looked at the mice who had gathered round to listen, then he said slowly, "THE CAT WILL BE SENT UP TO GET YOU!"

"The cat?" asked Gamey. "I think I saw the cat, and the cat saw me!" He turned to his mother. "Will the cat get me?" he asked.

"No, no, Gamey," said Mrs. Mouse. "But we must all be very quiet."

"No more swinging from the rafters, children," said Mr. Mouse.

"No more climbing up on chairs," he said to Gamey.

"I only wanted to see if snow had drifted over the land," said Gamey. "I wanted to see if Christmas was here."

"Christmas!" said Aunt Hettie. "If you don't stop the noise, the cat will get all of you long before Christmas!"

"Gamey thought it was snowing!" squeaked the attic mouse children. "He thinks that Christmas is here!" And they giggled and nudged each other until Uncle Roger said, "STOP IT!"

"Now," he said, when they had quieted down. "We kitchen mice have given this a great deal of thought. If that cat is ever brought into the house to clean out the mice in the attic, then he will certainly snoop around the kitchen as well."

"Yes," said Aunt Hettie. "And since that would mean the end for us too, we have decided that you attic mice have got to start wearing soft slippers on your feet."

The attic mice looked at one another. "Where will we get soft slippers?" asked Mrs. Mouse.

"You'll have to make them," said Aunt Hettie.

"But we have nothing to make them with," said Mr. Mouse.

"I'm sure you will think of something," said Uncle Roger, and he and Aunt Hettie left.

All that evening and the next day, the attic mouse

children tiptoed quietly about while their elders tried to think of something to make soft slippers with.

"We could make them out of newspapers," said Old Herbert.

"That's no good," said Mr. Mouse. "Newspapers crinkle and rustle and make more noise than bare feet."

"We could make them out of old rugs," said Ms. Gertrude.

"Oh, lovely!" said Mr. Timothy. "Then we would all have carpet slippers!"

"That won't do either," said Mrs. Mouse. "We have no old rugs to make them with."

Gamey was behind the sofa arranging pink and purple baubles.

I know what we could make the slippers out of, he said to himself. He crept into the box of decorations and lay down on the cotton snow. If real snow was drifting over the land and it really was Christmas, I wouldn't

have to make believe anymore. I would give my cotton snow away, and there would be slippers for everyone, and the cat wouldn't be sent up...oh, what am I going to do?

Gamey nestled into the cotton snow and closed his eyes. Suddenly he heard a voice say softly, "Gamey...Gamey Joe!" A tiny white mouse was sitting next to him. She was dressed all in white and shimmered like a snowflake. "Gamey Joe," she whispered. "If you give, you will have, and it truly will be Christmas!"

Gamey sat up and rubbed his eyes, but the tiny white mouse had disappeared. Gamey puzzled over what she had said for a while. Perhaps, he thought, if I give my cotton snow away, it really will be Christmas.

So Gamey took his cotton snow out of the box, and gave it to the attic mice. There was enough to make slippers for everyone. "And there's even enough to put a dab on the tip of your crutch," said Mr. Mouse.

"Oh, Gamey, thank you for the cotton snow," said Mrs. Mouse. "Now the people downstairs will never hear us."

All the attic mouse children were pleased with their slippers, and went sliding soundlessly over the attic floor.

"Let's play it's snowing, just like Gamey Joe does," said one. "We can make believe the slippers are snowshoes."

"Look at Gamey Joe now," said another. "He's cross-country skiing! Go, go, Gamey Joe!"

Gamey went schussing softly along, using his crutch as a ski pole. Everyone was as quiet as a mouse, and when Aunt Hettie and Uncle Roger came up from the kitchen, they were able to report there was no longer talk of sending the cat to the attic.

SILVER TINSEL

The days went by and Gamey watched and waited for Christmas. Each night he looked for the brightest star to shine in the sky. Each day he listened for mouse feet to squeak on the frosty ground. But instead of climbing up to see if snow had drifted over the land, he watched for snowflakes to float past the small window in the gable end of the attic.

Sometimes he thought of the tiny white mouse who had shimmered and disappeared. "If you give, you will have, and it truly will be Christmas," he whispered as he sat behind the sofa one wet rainy day. He shaped some tinsel into a silvery wreath and dangled blue spangles on it. "But I've waited and waited for Christmas," he said out loud. "WHEN WILL IT REALLY BE?"

"Ssh!" Mr. Mouse was looking up at a leak in the

ceiling right over the window. "When the wind whistles the squirrels off the roof, so we don't have to plug up the holes they've made," he said crossly. He wiped a raindrop off his nose. "Now stop sitting behind the sofa, son, and go ask your mother to bring a large pot."

Gamey Joe went schussing off in his soft slippers, poling along as fast as he could with his crutch. "Quick," he said to his mother. "There's a leak in the ceiling and we need a big pot."

"A leak!" said Aunt Hettie who was helping Mrs. Mouse with a new cake recipe.

"A leak!" said Uncle Roger, who had come along to sample the cake.

When they arrived with the pot, water was dripping onto the attic floor, PLIN PLINK, PLIN PLINK, PLIN PLINK, and a crowd had gathered round.

"Goodness," said Ms. Gertrude. "It does make a dreadful noise."

Mr. Mouse put the pot under the leak. The water dripped into the pot, PLUNK UN, PLUNK UN, PLUNK UN.

"Nasty sound," said Mr. Timothy.

"We'd better plug up that leak," said Old Herbert.

"Well," said Aunt Hettie, "you'd better plug it up fast. If the people downstairs hear that plinkity plunk, they'll be up to investigate in no time."

"And when they see all the queer tracks you've made with your slippers, they'll send up the cat right away," said Uncle Roger.

"Ssh! Listen," said Mrs. Mouse, and a hush fell over the attic.

Water had collected in the bottom of the pot. Now it made a different sound. PLIT PLAT, PLITTY KAT, KIT KAT, KITTY KAT, dripped the water.

Gamey covered his ears and crept behind the sofa.

"Oh, what are we going to do?" whispered Ms. Gertrude. "Whatever can we use for a plug?"

"You'll have to make one," said Aunt Hettie.

"But we have nothing to make it with," said Mrs. Mouse.

"I'm sure you will think of something," said Uncle Roger, and he and Aunt Hettie left.

"We've got to think of something, and we've got to think fast," said Mr. Mouse.

"We could make a plug with rags," said Old Herbert.

"Won't do," said Mrs. Mouse. "The water would leak through."

"We could stop it up with rocks," said Mr. Timothy.

"No good," said Mr. Mouse. "Can't shape a rock to fit."

"Should be something like a cork," said Ms. Gertrude.

"Something we can tamp in tight," said Mrs. Mouse.

Gamey looked at the silvery wreath he had shaped out of tinsel. He knew what they could use to stop up the leak. He closed his eyes. The water had reached the top of the pot and now it was making a new sound:

GLIB, GAMEY...GLUB, GAMEY...GAMEY, GAMEY...

The tiny white mouse was sitting next to him. She was dressed all in silver and sparkled like stardust.

"Gamey," she whispered. "If you give, you will have, and it truly will be Christmas!"

Gamey opened his eyes and rubbed them, but the tiny white mouse had faded away.

"Look!" said Mr. Mouse. "The water is about to spill over and we still don't have a plug!"

"Yes, we do," said Gamey, and he brought out all of his silvery tinsel.

"Oh, Gamey," said his mother. "This is just perfect. We can shape it to fit, and tamp it in tight!"

"Quick," said Mr. Mouse. "The water is spilling! We've got to get to the ceiling to plug up that hole, and not one of us can reach high enough to do it."

"I can do it," said Gamey. He climbed up the chair on top of the trunk, hooked his crutch over the windowsill, and hoisted himself up. But the hole was still too high. Gamey hesitated a moment. Then he hooked his crutch over the curved wooden frame of the window, and pulled himself up.

The attic mice didn't dare move while Gamey balanced on the edge of the frame and shaped the tinsel to fit the hole. Teetering on his tiptoes, he used his crutch to gently tamp the tinsel in tight. The water stopped dripping and there was silence.

REALLY CHRISTMAS

Ohhh!" the attic mice said. "Gamey's stopped up the leak!"

"Three cheers for Gamey!" cried the attic mouse children softly.

"Three cheers for Gamey Joe!"

As Gamey turned carefully to lower himself, he lost his balance and fell head first into the pot of water. The attic mice pulled him out and carried him to his bed, but though they tried and tried, they could not revive him.

Dr. Mouse was called up from the kitchen. After examining his little patient, he shook his head and said, "In a case like this, all you can do is make sure he has everything he wants, and hope for the best."

"We don't know what he wants," said Mr. Mouse.

"Yes, we do!" cried all the attic mouse children. "He wants it to be Christmas! He wants the snow to fall!"

Dr. Mouse stroked his whiskers and looked thoughtful. Finally he said, "In a case like this, all you can do is hope snow will fall." And he left.

Mrs. Mouse said sadly, "It's only just summer. How can we hope snow will fall?"

"We have to *make* the snow fall," said Mr. Mouse.

The attic mouse children looked at each other. "We'll find a way to make the snow fall," they said. And they went into a corner to think.

All that night Mr. and Mrs. Mouse watched over Gamey. But though his eyelids flickered once or twice, and his whiskers quivered, he lay still and did not speak.

"He's as quiet as a little mouse," said Aunt Hettie when she came up from the kitchen in the morning. And the cousin mice who had come up with her stared down at Gamey Joe's pale face and closed eyes.

"Hmmp," said Uncle Roger. He blew his nose very hard.

All that day, while it rained and rained, the attic mouse children sat in a corner whispering and thinking. In the evening, when the rain stopped and the moon came out, silence settled over the attic and the mouse children came out of the corner.

"We can do it!" they cried softly. "We'll save Gamey Joe the way Gamey saved us!"

And that is what they did. The attic mouse children tied their cotton snow slippers to long strands of tinsel. Then they used Gamey's crutch to hoist themselves onto the windowsill and unplug the hole in the roof. Holding the strands carefully, they hooked the crutch over the edge of the hole and climbed up onto the roof.

"Now," they called down softly, "move Gamey's bed over to the window." And they dangled their cotton snow slippers from the long strands of tinsel right over the edge of the roof.

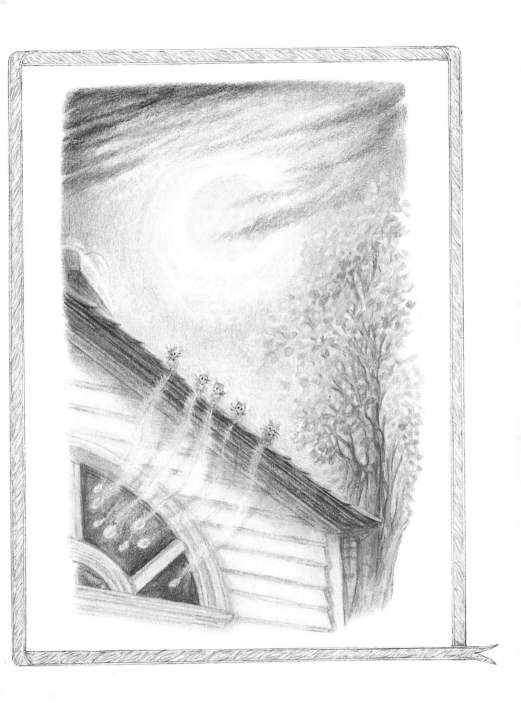

"Oooo...hhh," breathed the mice in the attic. For in the window, dancing and drifting and floating in the moonlight, were shimmering cotton snowflakes.

"Gamey," said his mother softly, "Gamey Joe. Open your eyes and see the snow fall."

Gamey's eyelids flickered and his whiskers quivered.

"See the snow fall, Gamey, see the snow fall," said the attic mice.

Gamey's whiskers quivered again, and from faraway the attic mice heard him say, "Listen, oh, listen. I hear mouse feet squeaking on the frosty ground!"

"Yes, Gamey, yes," the attic mice said, though they knew it was only the barefooted mouse children scampering on the roof.

Gamey Joe's eyelids flickered and his eyes opened.

"Look!" he said. "The brightest star of all is shining in the sky!"

The attic mice turned and looked. "Yes, Gamey," they said, though they knew it was only the moonlight dancing on the shining strands of tinsel.

Gamey's eyes opened wider. "Oh," he said, "snow is drifting over the land, and it is Christmas at last!"

"Yes, Gamey, yes." The tiny white mouse was sitting next to him. She was dressed all in moonbeams and gleamed and flashed like a diamond. "Yes, Gamey," she said. "It really is Christmas at last!"

Gamey Joe sat up and rubbed his eyes.

"Merry Christmas, Gamey Joe," sang out all the attic mice. "Merry Christmas!"

It was morning and the attic was abloom with roses that the little cousin mice had brought up from the garden. The attic mouse children had decked the roses with tinsel and bangles and baubles that twinkled and danced in the summer sunshine.

Gamey Joe rubbed his eyes again, and looked and looked.

"Merry Christmas!" sang the attic mouse children. And in that attic, it really was.